Love Poem to Ginger
& Other Poems

For Anna &
Rolfer —
Lovely party — 2013
& Happy New fear
Charley you
Mind Cer

B8708/
2013

Love Poem to Ginger

& Other Poems

Mộng Lan

ISBN: 978-0-9828227-1-5

Illustrations, cover photo, cover design by Mộng-Lan
Cover Art, detail from *Cherry Blossoms* and *Ginger & Basil,*
acrylic on canvas, 70 cm x 100 cm, 2012.

Published by Valiant Press
PO Box 2771
Sugar Land, Texas 77487

Books by Mộng-Lan
Song of the Cicadas (Juniper Prize)
Why is the Edge Always Windy?
Tango, Tangoing: Poems & Art
Tango, Tangueando: Poemas & Dibujos (bilingual Spanish-English edition)
Love Poem to Tofu & Other Poems (poetry & calligraphic art, chapbook)
Force of the Heart: Tango, Art (drawings, paintings)

for lovers of food

& my family

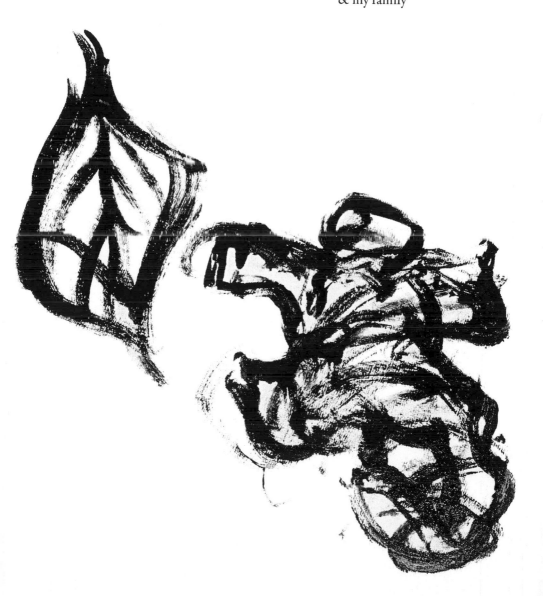

CONTENTS

ACKNOWLEDGEMENTS

Grateful acknowledgements to the editors of the following journals and literary magazines where my poems first appeared:

Asian American Literary Review, "Love poem to Nước Mắm"; "Love poem to Lemons"; "Love poem to Leeks."

Bayou, "Love Poem to Cherry Blossoms."

BN Magazine, "Straw Village, Humid Night."

Cerise Press, "Love Poem to Soto," www.cerisepress.com.

ISLE, "The Imperial Palace, Tokyo."

North American Review, "Love Poem to Phở."

Seattle Review, "Upon Seeing Marcel Marceau"; "Seoul Snow."

World Literature Today, "Love Poem to Garlic"; "Love Poem to Onion"; "Love Poem to Ginger"; "Love Poem to Basil."

Profound gratitude to my parents, especially my mother, for your support and for all the stories of our family, from those of my great grandparents to those of my grandparents. Deep appreciation to my family, mentors and friends all over the world for your loving support. Warm gratitude to David Shapiro for your kind words, support and friendship.

LOVE POEMS

Love Poem to Basil

in my garden i

       grow you

              Asian basil Italian basil

   a sweet scent

                  emanates

                lilting

   a leaf

      sings

Love Poem to Garlic

                    stinking rose
          the heady scent of you
                              tangy spicy
                                        most underrated
year-round orb
          bulbous root incandescent moon

invoked as deities by the Egyptians   garlic
                    each day with you is another day tripled

          stripped of your delicate covers your
                              fire-spitting fresh
                                        rawness

          i love you   unadulterated
                    a shiver once i bite you

medicinally you are a miracle
          fighting colds   blood thinner
                              anti-bacterial extraordinaire

          how to eat you raw   & love it:
peel the placenta-like cover
                              julienne
                    into fish sauce with red chili peppers lemon

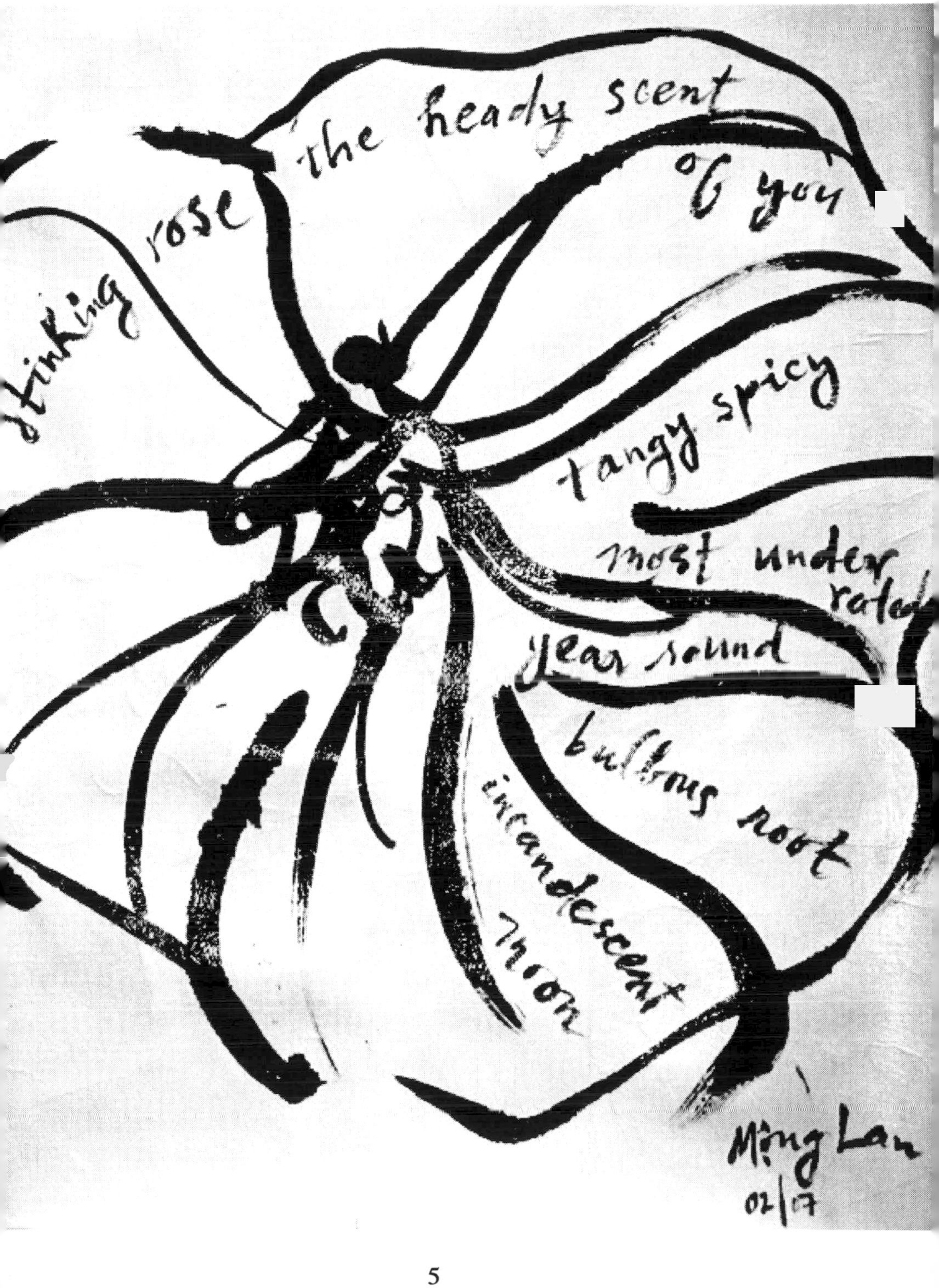

the heady scent
of you

stinking rose

tangy spicy

most under
rated

year round

bulbous root

incandescent
moon

Mộng Lan
02/17

5

your bold paleness exposed

                                     i imagine you

at every moment of everyday

Love Poem to Onion

the layers of you   how can i uncover?

allium cepa of the amaryllis family
succulent pungent bulb

peeling by hand
the layers of your skin
layers needed to delve into you

skirts your physical body
of your past
your soul

cut raw
to get to the very core of you

i dive into you
rivers in place

how to plummet how to sound out   the inner core?

you were powerful payment for builders
of the pyramids

as a child i planted you
watched your effervescent flowers

blow in the wind

                  then pulled you by the stalks

              erudite onion polyglot

                speaker of many cultures

      marinated in vinegar cut into triangles

in my grief i eat you whole

           purple yellow white

        multitudinous colors of you

                your many curvaceous smiles

bold orb   moon white as my whitest sheet

                your heart spotless

Love Poem to Leeks

plain sautéed with garlic   in soups   stir fries

                     whatever the mood   whatever the season

                   i fold you in

a sheaf of green   a sail of verdant thoughts

                  breezes   your warrior-like skin

i play on

     your stalks

verdant song of the earth   vital

    iron-rich   lovely your salient shoot

     sturdy accountable   you beam green from the ground

your tall leaves   O sheer ebullience

          like green sails

             swarthy deepness

                 verity itself

   bulbous protrusion

        fit sword

Love Poem to Lemons

of my desserts   lemon that fills my dreams

                           speaking to me in several

                             languages

               of my afternoons

        of my nights

into my glass of water   into olive oil

                    into soy sauce   nước mắm

into the bitterest   mildest   blandest concoctions

        i squeeze you into everything

        a fervent

           mirror

a sourness   brilliant as your color

                     your juice my lips pucker

        your rinds   i leave around to smell your vigor

bright burning desire

        liquid yellow like creativity

     your punch is great

             from a certain petiteness

     dense   but your glowingness expansive

as if acidic

     but actually alkaline

traveling through the body

famous detoxifier

delirious high C

trembling splash

squeaky thrill   nonchalant

gold   clear to the soul

Love Poem to Ginger

allayer of pain

zingiber officinale

strange root beige earth-lined

with sage wrinkles

wrangled

not with desire but to diffuse

desire

letting go —

this is how i let go of you

this is how

i let go

chop into small pieces

pour into water   simmer

until the juices come out

how i let go

swirling tremor

drink until your heart desires

soother

of despair

slaycr

O spicy rhizome!

Love Poem to Phở

yes, i am guilty

i am not a good Buddhist vegetarian
when in Sài Gòn or Hà Nội   i sometimes sneak bowls of you from
         the vendor
                        down the street   for fifty cents or less
    always without meat   bowls of phở clear fatless broth
                                            of chicken or beef

i sneak bowls of you past my other moral self
                        a secret sin   to remind me of days without pressure

                        without animal flesh i slurp you down
                                    only the perfume of you

i slurp you
            as Asians are wont to do   making noise to make
                        the taste sweeter
i slurp you with fresh
                cilantro lemon   mint leaves   dragon phở leaves

i slurp you with hot chili peppers tingling the tongue

                    fresh green peppers of memory penetrating
                                the palate

rice noodles   hanging over chopsticks ubiquitous legs

16

the Japanese say you have "a simple elegant taste"
         Vietnamese know you are never to be colonized

at home i make you with a vegetable broth
                              rice noodles & vegetables

     your broth   transparent   humble

Love Poem to Nước Mắm

O saucy
       little fish   packed in vats   limed with salt
                             pressed
pressed until your bones are worn into the salt water
         pressed until you no longer exist between the layers

until your essence of fish has been distilled   your protein extracted

            until the essence of your soul   released

how long to distill you
           from fish's bones
       into a tangy sauce that is essential to the Vietnamese
              all of Southeast Asia?

        from condiments to rice dishes to noodles
           your inner-most delights
     spiked with chilies   lemons

       how to let your inner soul fly?

         wayward demon   watery inner angel
              source of life

Love Poem to Soto

in Magelang the first time i hold
you   given to me by a kindly woman
        who laughs when i say "no a*yam*" ("no chicken")
i expect nothing

        you exist with such simplicity broth
                                clear as a daffodil day

        bean sprouts tofu   tempe cabbage shallots
rice from the verdant paddies of Java

                        it's love at first taste

the first bowl of you quenches a physical hunger

                        the second quenches the hunger
                                in my soul

from each spoonful the mountains of Java unfurl Gunung Merapi
                        lush bananas leaves beaconing
        jungles palm trees come forth
                        terraced rice paddies unroll
                                steppes of young strapling rice

with each spoonful Borodudur unfolds each carved stone story
                        each Buddha each stupta
        each memory of water & stone

21

                    yet to me
          how familiar
                    you are   your sweet juices

by what routes do i come to you?
                                        planes trains & buses

distances long & far away
          how long have i dreamt of you   distinct
                                        as the phở of my Việt Nam

                    the Javanese landscape glistens on your surface
your body swirling yellow with *kunyit* (tumeric)
                                        a dawning sun
O Soto dancing
                    on my tongue
                    how long have i dreamt of you?

For Komunitas Utan Kayu, with gratitude

Love Poem to Cherry Blossoms

kisses   rosy

inundating

with your labium

trunks arching deliver their generous sermons

blossoms swelling the earth's bosom   bursting

a row of cherry trees   every one of you

every petal snowing from branches

blooming you bless   legions to our faith

a moment   a largess translucent

in the snow of cherry

blossoms

[Tokyo 2003-2005]

The Imperial Palace
Tokyo

fish stroking

   the edges of the world

 little fetishes adorn cell phones

     transmitting messages mundane

     joyful & suicidal

in autumn the Imperial Palace robes itself in yellow & red trees

 while evergreens roam its slopes

   along the moat marathon

      runners gallop

       their muscles chiseled

   by their motions

   the most regal month yellow & red leaves enflame

    the grounds

living in one time zone permits us to see the praying

  mantis   climbing slowly stately

       the *little bitty boy*

   & his green scooter left crying

wild dogs on the hunt fierce as an arrow

   the Crown Princess sits &

     sighs from her window

Straw Village Humid Night

1

a young woman of 14   Bình An village   1947

what i remember   taunting sweet rain

i can't peel the humidity off
a few seconds being outdoors
mosquitoes bite me   mercilessly

i sip the thick air
heat so high i drown in it daily

some nights i lay awake
& dream of my future husband

our house we built from straw
the fields & clay
from river banks
we grow rice   rau muống   raise chickens
leeches suck
my ankles of blood
while i tend
the lilting rice shoots

2

when the French troops burst
            into our house at dusk my skin reacts an unbearable
                            stinging   my mind explodes

    brutality & lust in their eyes
                        frantically i run for
                        my life to the next village

                                    girls have been raped
                in such situations

    my father   a school principal
                            speaks
        nous ne sommes pas de genres militaires   nous ne combattons pas

            they don't touch him   perhaps for his white hair
                                perhaps for his French

    the soldiers (French sympathizers Africans
                    Vietnamese)   brusquely
            move & destroy   barbarity flickering in their eyes
            they haul my brothers to the base   pour
                            water
        into their moth
                        mouths

pulling them by the hair strings

                        my brothers'

                              jerking heads

      swallow the suffocating water

the soldiers kick

                    their bloated stomachs

         old tires

after my brothers trek
        back home   we destroy our house &
    move away from barbarity
          to Hà Nội   the city *civilisation*

i hear that they killed my uncles
        by what method i do not know

    we harbor in Hà Nội for several years
          until the newspapers say
              that the communists
        will take the north

Seoul Snow

smoky skeletons of trees

snow   ghostly   wet

Seoul awash in snow over buildings cars roads
                                        falling on the Han River

i wore a friend's mink coat something i could never afford
            nor want
                        (being alone
                                        poetry starts from here)

                                        city of bridges   extending forever
of quick deals industrious hustling for emails
                                        irons in the fire

thinking of Seoul's cold &

my friend's warmth her lack of English her expensive
                                        apartment overlooking the river
            the three cell phones she carries with her   the three
            packs of cigarettes she smokes a day

            smoke in cafés where women
                                        with mink coats go

smoke in her car smoke before lunch

during between

servings   & after

she writes of actors actresses   interviews them

they call her up

desiring interviews to make them

famous bloated like snow

smoke in traffic   Seoul rush hour

bumper to bumper smoke

Upon Seeing Marcel Marceau in Buenos Aires

speechless he was & will always be
>> not for words as he does not need them

>> a motion of the finger he lifts up the sun
>>>> chagrinned grin

under spotlight on the Teatro Grand Rex's stage in Buenos Aires
>> he mimes
>>>> as if on the humble streets of Paris

>> mining not for a *franc* but for Art
>>>> the hearts of those watching

>> one graceful gesture in complete silence
>>>> a complete paragraph

an old man becomes
>> splendidly young
>>>> nimble
>>>>> spritely
>> splendor in the spot-
>>> light

>> stuck in his bird
>>> cage his own heart
>>> hands flying like doves' wings leaving his body

a feminine motion of the hip   the eye smiles

goes through the motions
                    of a life   birth   youth middle age old age

in a court case   he is everybody
                                        at once judge
                        prosecutor defense victim perpetrator
                                            &   gets hanged

        flexibly humane

grand master of mimicry
                knowing too well the final fate of humanity
                                        of 84 years of living
                    & thus the last world tour

nothing remembered
                compares with
                                his deliberate hypnotic movements

                                        a single light

            a bird flies from his winged hands

NOTES

All paintings and drawings are the work of Mộng-Lan.

Page v, detail from *Ginger & Basil*, acrylic on canvas, 70 cm x 100 cm, 2012.

Pages 1-2, detail from *Ginger & Basil*, acrylic on canvas, 70 cm x 100 cm, 2012.

Page 5, *Love Poem to Garlic*, acrylic on canvas, 40 cm x 50 cm, 2012.

Page 9, *Onion*, pen & ink on paper, 28 cm x 35 cm, 2007.

Page 11, detail from *Lemons & Leeks*, acrylic on canvas, 70 cm x 100 cm, 2012.

Page 13, detail from *Lemons & Leeks*, acrylic on canvas, 70 cm x 100 cm, 2012.

Page 14, detail from *Ginger & Basil*, acrylic on canvas, 70 cm x 100 cm, 2012.

Page 17, *Love Poem to Phở*, acrylic on canvas, 40 cm x 50 cm.

Page 20, *School Ascending*, acrylic on canvas, 70 cm x 100 cm, 2012.

Page 21, *soto* is Indonesia's national dish, a traditional soup composed of broth, meat and vegetables. The ingredients of *soto* vary from region to region in Indonesia.

Page 24, detail from *Cherry Blossoms*, acrylic on canvas, 70 cm x 100 cm, 2012.

Page 26, detail from *Cherry Blossoms*, acrylic on canvas, 70 cm x 100 cm, 2012.

Page 28, *Binh An* means "peace" in Vietnamese.

Page 34, *Man*, 28 cm x 35 cm, pen & ink on paper, 2011.

Page 36, *Palomas*, 24 x 32, pen & ink on paper, 2012.

Page 38, *Face of Duality*, acrylic on canvas, 70 cm x 100 cm, 2012.

ABOUT THE AUTHOR

Vietnamese-born American poet, writer, painter, photographer, Argentine tango dancer, and educator, Mộng-Lan left her native Saigon on the last day of its evacuation. Mộng-Lan's first book of poems, *Song of the Cicadas* was awarded the Juniper Prize, the 2002 Great Lakes Colleges Association's New Writers Awards for Poetry, and was a finalist for the Poetry Society of America's Norma Farber Award. Her other books include *Why is the Edge Always Windy?*, *Tango, Tangoing: Poems & Art;* the bilingual Spanish-English edition, *Tango, Tangueando: Poemas & Dibujos; Love Poem to Tofu & Other Poems* (poetry & calligraphic art, chapbook); *Love Poem to Ginger & Other Poems: poetry & paintings* (chapbook). Mộng-Lan's poetry has been widely anthologized to include being in *Best American Poetry*; *The Pushcart Book of Poetry: Best Poems from 30 Years of the Pushcart Prize*; *Asian American Poetry: the Next Generation*; *Language for a New Century: Contemporary Poetry from the Middle East, Asia, and Beyond* (Norton); *Force Majeure* (Indonesia); *Black Dog, Black Night: Contemporary Vietnamese Poetry*; *Jungle Crows: a Tokyo Expatriate anthology*, and has appeared in leading American literary journals.

While still in high school, Mộng-Lan received scholarships to attend the Glassell School of Art in Houston for three years. Subsequently, her paintings and photographs have been exhibited for one year in the Capitol House in Washington D.C., in galleries in the United States, the Museum of Fine Arts in Houston, the Dallas Museum of Art, and in public exhibitions in Buenos Aires, Bali, Bangkok, Seoul and Tokyo. In conjunction with the National Endowment for the Arts, she was the Dallas Museum of Fine Arts' inaugural Visual Artist and Poet in Residence in 2005. An exhibition of her paintings and photographs, "The World of Mộng-Lan," ran for six months. Her book, *Force of the Heart: Tango, Art,* includes drawings and paintings that have for its focus the Argentine tango.

A Wallace Stegner Fellow in poetry for two years at Stanford University and a Fulbright Fellow in Vietnam, Mộng-Lan took her Master of Fine Arts at the University of Arizona. She has taught at the University of Arizona, Stanford University, and the University of Maryland in Tokyo. She also has given scores of readings and academic presentations in the United States, Argentina, Germany, Indonesia, Japan, Korea, Malaysia, Switzerland, Thailand, and Vietnam. Mộng-Lan travels frequently to give readings and lectures, show her artwork, teach and dance tango. Visit: www.monglan.com

Praise for Mộng-Lan's books:

On *Song of the Cicadas:*

"Welcome to a poetic voice that represents no less than a manifestation of soul. In Mộng-Lan's debut book, she has taken on the daunting responsibility of representing the Vietnamese nation and culture, via imagery, consciousness, and memory. Hers is a stunning experiment and a historical imperative."—**Jane Miller**

" In Asian tradition, poetry and visual art go hand in hand, with the collaboration of work, image, and calligraphy. Mộng-Lan's first book renews this tradition for American poetry, and with a startling subject matter.... From visual beauty, human suffering, and verbal inventiveness, Mộng-Lan stakes out a poetic territory that is completely her own."—**Alfred Corn**

On *Why Is The Edge Always Windy?*

" .... One should not be mislead by the title into thinking Mộng-Lan's work will be airy. The lyricism of her writing sings not of the ethereal but of a hard land; her work speaks not of arrested moments but of the tectonic force of history, which, moving at the pace of geological time, presses cultures against each other, folds moments over each other, edges everywhere and always exposed. Indeed, Mộng-Lan's are poems of exposure. Reading them is revelatory."— **Lyn Hejinian**

Mộng-Lan 's *Why Is The Edge Always Windy?* is a stunning book that turns our "era of exile" into one of lyric possession, the impulses to lament and to praise whirling together into a bittersweet music...."—**Alison Hawthorne Deming**

On *Tango, Tangoing: Poems & Art*

"A mesmerizing accomplishment - four voices at their climax: the dance, if we can call it that, the physics of being, the history and manual of dark beauty and the *voleos* of line, ink, stanza and voice, layers of loss, desire and the body in ecstatic explosions. Three drops of Lorca, one tincture of María Luisa Bombal and a full vasija of Mộng-Lan, a masterpiece, señores y señoras. A mathematics of fire."—**Juan Felipe Herrera**

" .... That Mộng-Lan succeeds at such an ambitious project in writing that is visually striking, musically complex, unabashedly erotic and deeply intelligent, is testimony to her very great poetic talents. This is a marvelous book, one I'll return to again and again."—**Kevin Prufer**